'To enter the country of age is a new experience, different from what you supposed it to be. Nobody, man or woman, knows the country until he has lived in it and has taken out his citizenship papers. Here is my own report, submitted as a road map and guide to some of the principal monuments.''

MALCOLM COWLEY grew up in Pittsburgh and interrupted his undergraduate career at Harvard to drive an ambulance during World War I. Mr. Cowley's *Exile's Return* was published in 1934, and his collected poems appeared in 1968. His most recent book, *The Dream of the Golden Mountains*, was published earlier this year.

Mr. Cowley's view of 80 is mostly from Sherman, Connecticut, where he lives with his wife Muriel.

Photograph on front of jacket
by Dudley Gray

 THE VIKING PRESS
625 Madison Avenue
New York, N.Y. 10022
PRINTED IN U.S.A.

ISBN 0-670-74614-2

THE VIEW FROM 80

Malcolm Cowley

THE VIKING PRESS
NEW YORK

First published in 1980 by The Viking Press
625 Madison Avenue, New York, N.Y. 10022
Published simultaneously in Canada by
Penguin Books Canada Limited

LIBRARY OF CONGRESS CATALOGING IN PUBLICATION DATA
Cowley, Malcolm, 1898–
The view from 80.
1. Cowley, Malcolm, 1898–   2. Aged—United
States—Biography. I. Title.
HQ1061.C663   305.2′6′0924   79-56286
ISBN 0-670-74614-2

A shorter version of *The View from 80* appeared originally
in *Life* magazine; "The Red Wagon" in *The Sewanee Review*.

Printed in the United States of America
Set in CRT Janson

Grateful acknowledgment is made to the following for permis-
sion to reprint copyrighted material:

Farrar, Straus and Giroux, Inc.: Selection from *Maximum Security Ward* by Ramon Guthrie. Copyright © 1968, 1969, 1970 by
Ramon Guthrie.

Alfred A. Knopf, Inc.: Excerpts from *The Measure of My Days*
by Florida Scott-Maxwell. Copyright © 1968 by Florida
Scott-Maxwell.

Macmillan Publishing Co., Inc., and A. P. Watt Ltd.: Selection
from "The Tower" from *Collected Poems* by William Butler
Yeats. Copyright 1928 by Macmillan Publishing Co., Inc., re-
newed 1956 by Georgie Yeats. Selection from "The Spur" from
Collected Poems by William Butler Yeats. Copyright 1940 by
Georgie Yeats, renewed 1968 by Bertha Georgie Yeats, Michael
Butler Yeats, and Anne Yeats.

A. P. Watt Ltd.: Selection from a letter by William Butler Yeats
to Lady Elizabeth Pelham, from Joseph Hone's *Life of W. B.
Yeats*, 1943.

To the Class of '19

A FOREWORD

Early that summer, Byron Dobell, then senior editor of the new monthly *Life*, phoned and asked whether I would like to write an article about growing old. I said I would think about it. The more I thought and read, over a period of weeks, the more I was attracted by the notion. Apparently a great deal had been written about old age, but most of the authors who dealt with it were lads and lasses, as it seemed to me, in their late fifties or early sixties. They knew the literature, but not the life. Some of them had brought together statistics or pored over medical reports, while others had tracked down the aged with camera and tape recorder; what they didn't and couldn't know was how it feels to be old. I knew, close as I was to my 80th birthday, and I decided that there was still room for an honest personal report.

I set to work. In writing about age I was delayed by some of the infirmities that were part of my subject. Phlebitis was the unexpected one; it had me on my back for much of August; and also there was that 80th-birthday celebration. Nevertheless the article was finished in good time to be published in the December 1978 number of *Life*. The response over the next few months was surprising. "The View from 80" won various awards (if two can be called various), it was condensed in *Reader's Digest*, and it called forth what was to me an astounding number of letters from many parts of the country.

Almost all the letters were from men and women in their eighties who spoke frankly about their sorrows and satisfactions. They gave me credit for being equally frank. Many were struck by a list I had made of messages from the body that tell us we are old. Thus, V. Woods Bailey wrote from Iowa, "I was chagrined to find that you were onto many of the dark secrets of my more than 80 years—especially the row of little bottles on the shelf. I have never before in all my life resorted to *pills*—and now here stands that little row. But on one point I am ahead—all this came on me after I was 85, instead of after I was 80." Morton S. Enslin, a classmate of 82 whom I had mentioned by name, wrote from Pennsylvania, "Those lists of messages were rather more than guesswork. Nearly all were too truly mine. And a couple of them I read with distinct pleasure and relief, for I had been inclined to view them as peculiarly mine."

Another classmate of 82, George D. Flynn, Jr., wrote from Providence, "Well, *did* we go for that December *Life* story! . . . Dot and I read it a couple of times and have quoted from it often, especially that item about your agelessness when sitting in a chair, ruminating and remembering, and then, what happens when you decide to get up for a ramble in the woods with gun and rod, creaking to a plantigrade position and almost falling on your butt." Claire Whitehurst of Coral Gables had no time for sitting back in a chair. "Being one year less than 80 and a lady," she said, "I view the panorama of life a bit differently—always busy, always searching for the new, which keeps my daughter and granddaughters busy keeping up with my new friends." Several correspondents were proud of being physically active, none prouder than A. M. Botway, then 86, who wrote from Key West, "I'm afraid that my new country"—that of age—"is not new to me. At seven this morning I did what I've been doing for at least 15 years, ever since I had to slow down. When I opened my eyes I did my 20 sit-ups while still on my back, jumped out of bed, slipped into my swim trunks, jumped on my bike and headed the half mile to the Atlantic, where I first did the very same calisthenics we did in the army when Pershing went after Pancho Villa in 1916.

"After the work-out I swam around till I had enough, jumped on the bike, and at 7:30 was enjoying a hearty breakfast. . . . Ponce de Leon, here I come."

Several letters that gave me a pleasant feeling were from women I had known as girls and hadn't seen for half a century. Jean Miller Davis wrote from Pittsburgh, where she has spent her life, "I could not resist the urge to tell you how much I enjoyed sharing your view, as I am now 81. In Peabody High School I sat just across the aisle from you in several classes and thought you were very smart. My life has been quite a happy one and I am the grandmother of 12. . . . *P.S.* I no longer have red hair—it is mostly gray now and my eyes are very poor." Mary Mardis Davis wrote me from Ohio. Nine years older than I, she was the daughter of a prosperous farmer; I knew her when she was the prettiest girl in our little Pennsylvania village. Once when she was 20 and came to dinner, she so embarrassed me with her good looks that I crawled under the dining-room table, among all those feet.

Mary became a nurse and married a Kentucky doctor. While her husband was in the army during World War I, she ran an emergency hospital with 150 beds and no other nurses to help her. She has spent most of her life taking care of other people. In 1945, when her husband died of a heart attack, the other doctors in the county—there weren't many of them—persuaded her to keep his office open and take care of the patients—"as I had been doing," she says. "They checked all the medicines and said they would stand back of me. After two years, making calls at night way out in the country was too much for me and I sold my home." She now lives with a daughter near Columbus and she writes, "I am 89 and you really hit the nail on the head. I can't hear. I don't use a cane, but should. I read all the time and I'm not seeing too well. But I am with my daughter and she allows me to do as I please, and I am getting along fine." Mary has started to put her memories on tape.

Lois Blair Jensen is also older than I. In school days my friend was her younger sister Mary Blair, who became a leading lady on Broadway and died of TB. Lois is now in a Pennsylvania nursing home. "After lunch," she writes, "nephew Kenneth Blair brought me a copy of *Life* and read a part aloud to me. My eyes are not good. I enjoyed the photos. May I congratulate you on being 80. I am 86. Before lunch I had told the visiting doctor that I consider Golden Age as Yuk." She was not the only correspondent who objected to the phrase Golden Age. On a related topic, Dorothy Shelmire, 83, was rather heavily ironic. "Maybe—just *maybe*—" she wrote from a town near Philadelphia, "I might in the future *profit* from your article and learn to *appreciate* the pleasures (?) of being past 80!?"

A letter signed only "Gracie"—it must have

been from Gracie Carlisle, whom I haven't seen since the 1930s—berated me for being a slippered pantaloon. She said, "This is in commiseration of your 'Creaking Age Speaks.' You're as old as you FEEL. Old age is just a rumor." Gracie has often shown her spunk, and I bowed my head to her rebuke. I was flattered, though, by a letter from Ida Carey, who wrote from Mt. Pleasant, Michigan, "I *love* your article, which 'hits the nail on the head' for me. I find, in these last several months, that it takes sheer *will power* to get up from a sitting position. Once up, I walk around these rooms bent forward (due to arthritis) till I must resemble that slouch that Groucho Marx used to assume. At 90, my contemporaries are gone, but having lived in this community for 70 years, I have many good friends. Have my own teeth (a few missing molars) and can recite *reams* of poetry.... You have inspired me to begin writing a sort of memoir of my life—something my elder daughter, Pat, had asked me many times to do."

There should be more, many more, of such memoirs. Each of the letters that came to me— and I might have quoted from dozens of others— somehow asserted a different personality, and many of them gave hints of lifetimes rich in adventures. Rereading the letters after several months, I felt a burst of affection for those in my age group; for all my coevals, to use a word from "the literature." Each of them has found his or her own sort of wisdom, an individual way of adjusting to circumstances, and some have displayed a courage that puts me to shame. We octogenarians form a loose and large secret order, with many members in each city and with representatives in almost every village. I have to say members and representatives, not chapters, for most of us are comparatively isolated (except for our families, if we are lucky enough to have them). I should like to establish communication and to be, in some measure, a spokesman for others. If I had time I should enjoy writing a long letter to each of the volunteer correspondents, and to many more besides. But after 80 there is never time enough.

Instead of writing letters, I set to work on this little book. I planned to include in it everything said in the article, besides much else for which I hadn't found space. Still other reflections, examples, anecdotes crowded in on me as I worked ahead. The manuscript grew longer, but without going beyond the modest limits I had set for it. Here is the book, and I hope it will serve as a personal message to each of my comrades in age.

M.C.

THE
VIEW
FROM
80

They gave me a party on my 80th birthday in August 1978. First there were cards, letters, telegrams, even a cable of congratulation or condolence; then there were gifts, mostly bottles; there was catered food and finally a big cake with, for some reason, two candles (had I gone back to very early childhood?). I blew the candles out a little unsteadily. Amid the applause and clatter I thought about a former custom of the Northern Ojibwas when they lived on the shores of Lake Winnipeg. They were kind to their old people, who remembered and enforced the ancient customs of the tribe, but when an old person became decrepit, it was time for him to go. Sometimes he was simply abandoned, with a little food, on an island in the lake. If he deserved special honor, they held a tribal feast for him. The old man sang a death song and danced, if he could. While he was still singing, his son came from behind and brained him with a tomahawk.

That was quick, it was dignified, and I wonder whether it was any more cruel, essentially, than some of our civilized customs or inadvertences in disposing of the aged. I believe in rites and ceremonies. I believe in big parties for special occasions such as an 80th birthday. It is a sort of belated bar mitzvah, since the 80-year-old, like a Jewish adolescent, is entering a new stage of life; let him (or her) undergo a *rite de passage*, with toasts and a cantor. Seventy-year-olds, or septuas, have the illusion of being middle-aged, even if they have been pushed back on a shelf. The 80-year-old, the octo, looks at the double-dumpling figure and admits that he is old. The last act has begun, and it will be the test of the play.

He has joined a select minority that numbers, in this country, 4,842,000 persons (according to Census Bureau estimates for 1977), or about two percent of the American population. Two-thirds of the octos are women, who have retained the good habit of living longer than men. Someday you, the reader, will join that minority, if you escape hypertension and cancer, the two killers, and if you survive the dangerous years from 75 to 79, when half the survivors till then are lost. With advances in medicine, the living space taken over by octos is growing larger year by year.

To enter the country of age is a new experience, different from what you supposed it to be. Nobody, man or woman, knows the country until he has lived in it and has taken out his citizenship papers. Here is my own report, submitted as a road map and guide to some of the principal monuments.

THE new octogenarian feels as strong as ever when he is sitting back in a comfortable chair. He ruminates, he dreams, he remembers. He doesn't want to be disturbed by others. It seems to him that old age is only a costume assumed for those others; the true, the essential self is ageless. In a moment he will rise and go for a ramble in the woods, taking a gun along, or a fishing rod, if it is spring. Then he creaks to his feet, bending forward to keep his balance, and realizes that he will do nothing of the sort. The body and its surroundings have their messages for him, or only one message: "You are old." Here are some of the occasions on which he receives the message:

——when it becomes an achievement to do thoughtfully, step by step, what he once did instinctively

——when his bones ache

——when there are more and more little bottles in the medicine cabinet, with instructions for taking four times a day

——when he fumbles and drops his toothbrush (butterfingers)

——when his face has bumps and wrinkles, so that he cuts himself while shaving (blood on the towel)

——when year by year his feet seem farther from his hands

——when he can't stand on one leg and has trouble pulling on his pants

——when he hesitates on the landing before walking down a flight of stairs

——when he spends more time looking for things misplaced than he spends using them after he (or more often his wife) has found them

——when he falls asleep in the afternoon

——when it becomes harder to bear in mind two things at once

——when a pretty girl passes him in the street and he doesn't turn his head

——when he forgets names, even of people he saw last month ("Now I'm beginning to forget nouns," the poet Conrad Aiken said at 80)

——when he listens hard to jokes and catches everything but the snapper

——when he decides not to drive at night anymore

——when everything takes longer to do—bathing, shaving, getting dressed or undressed—but when time passes quickly, as if he were gathering speed while coasting downhill. The year from 79 to 80 is like a week when he was a boy.

Those are some of the intimate messages. "Put cotton in your ears and pebbles in your shoes," said a gerontologist, a member of that new profession dedicated to alleviating all maladies of old people except the passage of years. "Pull on rubber gloves. Smear Vaseline over your glasses, and there you have it: instant aging." Not quite. His formula omits the messages from the social world, which are louder, in most cases, than those from within. We start by growing old in other people's eyes, then slowly we come to share their judgment.

I remember a morning many years ago when I was backing out of the parking lot near the railroad station in Brewster, New York. There was a near collision. The driver of the other car jumped out and started to abuse me; he had his fists ready. Then he looked hard at me and said, "Why, you're an old man." He got back into his car, slammed the door, and drove away, while I stood there fuming. "I'm only 65," I thought. "He wasn't driving carefully. I can still take care of myself in a car, or in a fight, for that matter."

My hair was whiter—it may have been in 1974—when a young woman rose and offered me her seat in a Madison Avenue bus. That message was kind and also devastating. "Can't I even stand up?" I thought as I thanked her and declined the seat. But the same thing happened twice the following year, and the second time I gratefully accepted the offer, though with a sense of having diminished myself. "People are right about me," I thought while wondering why all those kind gestures were made by women. Do men now regard themselves as the weaker sex, not called upon to show consideration? All the same it was a relief to sit down and relax.

A few days later I wrote a poem, "The Red Wagon," that belongs in the record of aging:

For his birthday they gave him a red express
    wagon
with a driver's high seat and a handle that
    steered.
His mother pulled him around the yard.
"Giddyap," he said, but she laughed and went
    off
to wash the breakfast dishes.

"I wanta ride too," his sister said,
and he pulled her to the edge of a hill.
"Now, sister, go home and wait for me,
but first give a push to the wagon."

He climbed again to the high seat,
this time grasping the handle-that-steered.
The red wagon rolled slowly down the slope,
then faster as it passed the schoolhouse
and faster as it passed the store,
the road still dropping away.
Oh, it was fun.

But would it ever stop?
Would the road always go downhill?

The red wagon rolled faster.
Now it was in strange country.
It passed a white house he must have dreamed
  about,
deep woods he had never seen,
a graveyard where, something told him, his
  sister was buried.

Far below
the sun was sinking into a broad plain.

The red wagon rolled faster.
Now he was clutching the seat, not even trying
  to steer.
Sweat clouded his heavy spectacles.
His white hair streamed in the wind.

EVEN before he or she is 80, the aging person
may undergo another identity crisis like that of
adolescence. Perhaps there had also been a middle-aged crisis, the male or the female menopause,
but for the rest of adult life he had taken himself
for granted, with his capabilities and failings.
Now, when he looks in the mirror, he asks himself, "Is this really me?"—or he avoids the mirror
out of distress at what it reveals, those bags and
wrinkles. In his new makeup he is called upon to
play a new role in a play that must be improvised.
André Gide, that long-lived man of letters, wrote
in his journal, "My heart has remained so young
that I have the continual feeling of playing a part,

the part of the 70-year-old that I certainly am; and the infirmities and weaknesses that remind me of my age act like a prompter, reminding me of my lines when I tend to stray. Then, like the good actor I want to be, I go back into my role, and I pride myself on playing it well."

In his new role the old person will find that he is tempted by new vices, that he receives new compensations (not so widely known), and that he may possibly achieve new virtues. Chief among these is the heroic or merely obstinate refusal to surrender in the face of time. One admires the ships that go down with all flags flying and the captain on the bridge.

Among the vices of age are avarice, untidiness, and vanity, which last takes the form of a craving to be loved or simply admired. Avarice is the worst of those three. Why do so many old persons, men and women alike, insist on hoarding money when they have no prospect of using it and even when they have no heirs? They eat the cheapest food, buy no clothes, and live in a single room when they could afford better lodging. It may be that they regard money as a form of power; there is a comfort in watching it accumulate while other powers are dwindling away. How often we read of an old person found dead in a hovel, on a mattress partly stuffed with bankbooks and stock certificates! The bankbook syndrome, we call it in our family, which has never succumbed.

Untidiness we call the Langley Collyer syndrome. To explain, Langley Collyer was a former concert pianist who lived alone with his 70-year-old brother in a brownstone house on upper Fifth Avenue. The once fashionable neighborhood had become part of Harlem. Homer, the brother, had been an admiralty lawyer, but was now blind and partly paralyzed; Langley played for him and fed him on buns and oranges, which he thought would restore Homer's sight. He never threw away a daily paper because Homer, he said, might want to read them all. He saved other things as well and the house became filled with rubbish from roof to basement. The halls were lined on both sides with bundled newspapers, leaving narrow passageways in which Langley had devised booby traps to catch intruders.

On March 21, 1947, some unnamed person telephoned the police to report that there was a dead body in the Collyer house. The police broke down the front door and found the hall impassable; then they hoisted a ladder to a second-story window. Behind it Homer was lying on the floor in a bathrobe; he had starved to death. Langley had disappeared. After some delay, the police broke into the basement, chopped a hole in the roof, and began throwing junk out of the house, top and bottom. It was 18 days before they found Langley's body, gnawed by rats. Caught in one of his own booby traps, he had died in a hallway just outside Homer's door. By that time the police had collected, and the Department of Sanitation had hauled away, 120 tons of rubbish, including, besides the newspapers, 14 grand pianos and the parts of a dismantled Model T Ford.

Why do so many old people accumulate junk, not on the scale of Langley Collyer, but still in a dismaying fashion? Their tables are piled high with it, their bureau drawers are stuffed with it, their closet rods bend with the weight of clothes not worn for years. I suppose that the piling up is partly from lethargy and partly from the feeling that everything once useful, including their own bodies, should be preserved. Others, though not so many, have such a fear of becoming Langley Collyers that they strive to be painfully neat. Every tool they own is in its place, though it will never be used again; every scrap of paper is filed away in alphabetical order. At last their immoderate neatness becomes another vice of age, if a milder one.

THE vanity of older people is an easier weakness to explain, and to condone. With less to look forward to, they yearn for recognition of what they have been: the reigning beauty, the athlete, the soldier, the scholar. It is the beauties who have the hardest time. A portrait of themselves at twenty hangs on the wall, and they try to resemble it by making an extravagant use of creams, powders, and dyes. Being young at heart, they think they are merely revealing their essential persons. The athletes find shelves for their silver trophies, which are polished once a year. Perhaps a letter sweater lies wrapped in a bureau drawer. I remember one evening when a no-longer athlete had guests for dinner and tried to find his sweater. "Oh, that old thing," his wife said. "The moths got into it and I threw it away." The athlete sulked and his guests went home early.

Often the yearning to be recognized appears in conversation as an innocent boast. Thus, a distinguished physician, retired at 94, remarks casually that a disease was named after him. A former judge bursts into chuckles as he repeats bright things that he said on the bench. Aging scholars complain in letters (or one of them does), "As I approach 70 I'm becoming avid of honors, and such things—medals, honorary degrees, etc.—are only passed around among academics on a *quid pro quo* basis (one hood capping another)." Or they say querulously, "Bill Underwood has ten honorary doctorates and I have only three. Why didn't they elect me to . . . ?" and they mention the name of some learned society. That search for honors is a harmless passion, though it may lead to jealousies and deformations of character, as with Robert Frost in his later years. Still, honors cost little. Why shouldn't the very old have more than their share of them?

To be admired and praised, especially by the young, is an autumnal pleasure enjoyed by the lucky ones (who are not always the most deserving). "What is more charming," Cicero observes in his famous essay *De Senectute*, "than an old age surrounded by the enthusiasm of youth! . . . Attentions which seem trivial and conventional are marks of honor—the morning call, being sought after, precedence, having people rise for you, being escorted to and from the forum. . . . What pleasures of the body can be compared to the prerogatives of influence?" But there are also pleasures of the body, or the mind, that are enjoyed by a greater number of older persons.

Those pleasures include some that younger people find hard to appreciate. One of them is simply sitting still, like a snake on a sun-warmed stone, with a delicious feeling of indolence that was seldom attained in earlier years. A leaf flutters down; a cloud moves by inches across the horizon. At such moments the older person, completely relaxed, has become a part of nature—and a living part, with blood coursing through his veins. The future does not exist for him. He thinks, if he thinks at all, that life for younger persons is still a battle royal of each against each, but that now he has nothing more to win or lose. He is not so much above as outside the battle, as if he had assumed the uniform of some small neutral country, perhaps Liechtenstein or Andorra. From a distance he notes that some of the

combatants, men or women, are jostling ahead—
but why do they fight so hard when the most
they can hope for is a longer obituary? He can
watch the scrounging and gouging, he can hear
the shouts of exultation, the moans of the gravely
wounded, and meanwhile he feels secure; nobody
will attack him from ambush.

Age has other physical compensations besides
the nirvana of dozing in the sun. A few of the
simplest needs become a pleasure to satisfy.
When an old woman in a nursing home was asked
what she really liked to do, she answered in one
word: "Eat." She might have been speaking for
many of her fellows. Meals in a nursing home,
however badly cooked, serve as climactic moments of the day. The physical essence of the
pensioners is being renewed at an appointed
hour; now they can go back to meditating or to
watching TV while looking forward to the next
meal. They can also look forward to sleep, which
has become a definite pleasure, not the mere in-
terruption it once had been.

Here I am thinking of old persons under nursing care. Others ferociously guard their independence, and some of them suffer less than one
might expect from being lonely and impover-
ished. They can be rejoiced by visits and meetings, but they also have company inside their
heads. Some of them are busiest when their hands
are still. What passes through the minds of many
is a stream of persons, images, phrases, and famil-

iar tunes. For some that stream has continued since childhood, but now it is deeper; it is their present and their past combined. At times they conduct silent dialogues with a vanished friend, and these are less tiring—often more rewarding—than spoken conversations. If inner resources are lacking, old persons living alone may seek comfort and a kind of companionship in the bottle. I should judge from the gossip of various neighborhoods that the outer suburbs from Boston to San Diego are full of secretly alcoholic widows. One of those widows, an old friend, was moved from her apartment into a retirement home. She left behind her a closet in which the floor was covered wall to wall with whiskey bottles. "Oh, those empty bottles!" she explained. "They were left by a former tenant."

Not whiskey or cooking sherry but simply giving up is the greatest temptation of age. It is something different from a stoical acceptance of infirmities, which is something to be admired. At 63, when he first recognized that his powers were failing, Emerson wrote one of his best poems, "Terminus":

> It is time to be old,
> To take in sail:—
> The god of bounds,
> Who sets to seas a shore,
> Came to me in his fatal rounds,
> And said: "No more!
> No farther shoot

Thy broad ambitious branches, and thy root.
Fancy departs: no more invent;
Contract thy firmament
To compass of a tent."

Emerson lived in good health to the age of 79. Within his narrowed firmament, he continued working until his memory failed; then he consented to having younger editors and collaborators. The givers-up see no reason for working. Sometimes they lie in bed all day when moving about would still be possible, if difficult. I had a friend, a distinguished poet, who surrendered in that fashion. The doctors tried to stir him to action, but he refused to leave his room. Another friend, once a successful artist, stopped painting when his eyes began to fail. His doctor made the mistake of telling him that he suffered from a fatal disease. He then lost interest in everything except the splendid Rolls-Royce, acquired in his prosperous days, that stood in the garage. Daily he wiped the dust from its hood. He couldn't drive it on the road any longer, but he used to sit in the driver's seat, start the motor, then back the Rolls out of the garage and drive it in again, back twenty feet and forward twenty feet; that was his only distraction.

I haven't the right to blame those who surrender, not being able to put myself inside their minds or bodies. Often they must have compelling reasons, physical or moral. Not only do they suffer from a variety of ailments, but also they are made to feel that they no longer have a function in the community. Their families and neighbors don't ask them for advice, don't really listen when they speak, don't call on them for efforts. One notes that there are not a few recoveries from apparent senility when that situation changes. If it doesn't change, old persons may decide that efforts are useless. I sympathize with their problems, but the men and women I envy are those who accept old age as a series of challenges.

For such persons, every new infirmity is an enemy to be outwitted, an obstacle to be overcome by force of will. They enjoy each little victory over themselves, and sometimes they win a major success. Renoir was one of them. He continued painting, and magnificently, for years after he was crippled by arthritis; the brush had to be strapped to his arm. "You don't need your hand to paint," he said. Goya was another of the unvanquished. At 72 he retired as an official painter of the Spanish court and decided to work only for himself. His later years were those of the famous "black paintings" in which he let his imagination run (and also of the lithographs, then a new technique). At 78 he escaped a reign of terror in Spain by fleeing to Bordeaux. He was deaf and his eyes were failing; in order to work he had to wear several pairs of spectacles, one over another, and then use a magnifying glass; but he was producing splendid work in a totally new style. At 80 he drew an ancient man propped on two sticks, with a mass of white hair and beard hiding his face and with the inscription "I am still learning."

Giovanni Papini said when he was nearly blind, "I prefer martyrdom to imbecility." After writing sixty books, including his famous *Life of Christ*, he was at work on two huge projects when he was stricken with a form of muscular atrophy. He lost the use of his left leg, then of his fingers, so that he couldn't hold a pen. The two big books, though never to be finished, moved forward slowly by dictation; that in itself was a triumph. Toward the end, when his voice had become incomprehensible, he spelled out a word, tapping on the table to indicate letters of the alphabet. One hopes never to be faced with the need for such heroic measures.

"Eighty years old!" the great Catholic poet Paul Claudel wrote in his journal. "No eyes left, no ears, no teeth, no legs, no wind! And when all is said and done, how astonishingly well one does without them!"

YEATS is the great modern poet of age, though he died—I am now tempted to say—as a mere stripling of 73. His reaction to growing old was not that of a stoic like Emerson or Cicero, bent on obeying nature's laws and the edicts of Terminus, the god "Who sets to seas a shore"; it was that of a

romantic rebel, the Faustian man. He was only 61
when he wrote (in "The Tower"):

> What shall I do with this absurdity—
> O heart, O troubled heart—this caricature,
> Decrepit age that has been tied to me
> As to a dog's tail?

At 68 he began to be worried because he wasn't
producing many new poems. Could it be, he must
have wondered, that his libido had lost its force
and that it was somehow connected with his
imagination? He had the Faustian desire for renewed youth, felt almost universally, but in
Yeats's case with a stronger excuse, since his
imagination was the center of his life. A friend
told him, with gestures, about Dr. Steinach's then
famous operation designed to rejuvenate men by
implanting new sex glands. The operation has
since fallen into such medical disfavor that Steinach's name is nowhere mentioned in the latest
edition of *The Encyclopaedia Britannica*. But
Yeats read a pamphlet about it in the Trinity
College library, in Dublin, and was favorably
impressed. After consulting a physician, who
wouldn't say yes or no, he arranged to have the
operation performed in a London clinic; that was
in May 1934.

Back in Dublin he felt himself to be a different
man. Oliver St. John Gogarty, himself a physician, reports a conversation with Yeats that took
place the following summer. "I was horrified," he

says, "to hear when it was too late that he had undergone such an operation. 'On both sides?' I asked.

" 'Yes,' he acknowledged.

" 'But why on earth did you not consult anyone?'

" 'I read a pamphlet.'

" 'What was wrong with you?'

" 'I used to fall asleep after lunch.' "

It was no use making a serious answer to Gogarty the jester. He tells us in his memoir of Yeats that the poet claimed to have been greatly benefited by the operation, but adds, "I have reason to believe that this was not so. He had reached the age when he would not take 'Yes' for an answer." Gogarty's judgment as a physician was probably right; the poet's physical health did not improve and in fact deteriorated. One conjectures that the operation may have put an added strain on his heart and thus may have shortened his life by years. Psychologically, however, Yeats was transformed. He began to think of himself as "the wild old wicked man," and in that character he wrote dozens of poems in a new style, direct, earthy, and passionate. One of them reads:

You think it horrible that lust and rage
Should dance attention upon my old age;
They were not such a plague when I was
    young;
What else have I to spur me into song?

False remedies are sometimes beneficial in their own fashion. What artist would not sacrifice a few years of life in order to produce work on a level with Yeats's *Last Poems*? Early in January 1939, he wrote to his friend Lady Elizabeth Pelham:

> I know for certain that my time will not be long. . . . I am happy, and I think full of energy, of an energy I had despaired of. It seems to me that I have found what I wanted. When I try to put all into a phrase I say, "Man can embody truth but he cannot know it." I must embody it in the completion of my life.

His very last poem, and one of the best, is "The Black Tower," dated the 21st of that month. Yeats died a week after writing it.

2

One's 80th birthday is a time for thinking about the future, not the past. From Census Bureau reports I learned that in August 1978, as a white male, I had a life expectancy of 6.7 years; it would have been 8.6 years if I were a woman and 11.0 years if I were a black woman. There was something unfair in those figures, I thought in my sexist fashion. Women have generally lived longer than men (as the females of almost all the higher mammals do), but lately the difference in years has been pretty steadily growing. In 1920 there was only a 1.0-year difference between the life expectancy of a newborn male and that of a newborn female (according to the Census Bureau, whose records were incomplete at the time). By 1940 the difference had increased to 4.4 years (with more complete reporting), by 1960 to 6.5 years, and by 1977 to 7.8 years (68.7 for men, 76.5 for women). Why the disparity? It can be argued that men have been dying sooner than women partly because they were exposed to greater strains in their active lives and partly because of problems connected with retirement; housewives never retire. But now that more and more women are fighting to rise in the business world; now that more of them smoke and drink like troopers, will the difference be as great as before? I wonder.

For "Negro and Other" the life expectancy at birth has always been lower than for whites. Here the difference, largely due to lower incomes for blacks, was 9.6 years in 1900, but it has been decreasing; the Census Bureau reports that it has come down to 5.3 years. After 80, for some reason, black males and black females both live longer than their white counterparts. As I write, the oldest person in the United States is a former slave, Charlie Smith, who was kidnapped near the Liberian coast and sold in the New Orleans slave market in 1854, at the age of 12. Much later he worked in an orange grove until he was 113; then he was retired because people thought he was too old to climb trees. In the fall of 1978, when he was 136 years old by Social Security records, a television crew set up sound equipment at the retirement home where he was living in Bartow, Florida, but they reported that he couldn't be understood; he mumbled. Nature sets a limit on our effective lives, even for persons of exceptional vitality such as Charlie Smith.[1]

Vitalism—the notion that we live until we exhaust our vital energy—is medically discredited, but I'm not sure that the doctors are right. Sometimes I feel that each of us is born with a smaller or larger store of energy; the differences can be observed even in very young babies. Of course the store isn't constant; it can be renewed or diminished by circumstances; but each of us may have some voice in determining how fast the energy will be spent. One of Hemingway's heroes says of himself on his deathbed, "He had sold vitality, in one form or another, all his life." Hemingway too sold vitality, or tossed it away. Before he was 62, the shelves in his store were empty. Many years ago the younger partners of J. P. Morgan, Sr., were deciding, when they accepted the offer of partnership, that they would lead short, frenzied lives and make a lot of money. I heard that some of their widows lived in

---

[1] Smith died at the Bartow Convalescent Center in October 1979, when according to Social Security records he was 137. His age has been disputed by the editor of the *Guinness Book of World Records*, who asserts that Smith was only 104. That lower figure, if accepted, would make him younger than many other Americans. In June 1979 Social Security payments were being made to 11,885 persons of 100 or older.

brownstone houses near the Morgan mansion on Murray Hill.

Elihu Root, the internationalist, chose a different course. He decided at the age of 47 to last a long time (or so he afterward confided to one of his physicians, who passed along the word to me much later). From that day forward he watched his diet and refrained from activities that would strain his heart, such, for instance, as running for office (though he consented to serve as secretary of state and later as U.S. senator, in the days when senators were still appointed). He was always the wise counselor, not the harassed executive, and he lived to be just short of 92. John D. Rockefeller, Sr., appears to have made a similar decision at 58, after he had amassed his fortune; thenceforth he devoted himself to golf and philanthropy. He wasn't a philanthropist on the links. The only time of record that he tipped his caddy more than a dime was during the bank holiday of 1933, when dimes were scarcer than dollars. But his public benefactions were enormous, and he had given away $530 million before he died at 97.

The doctors haven't had much success in lengthening the maximum life span of the human species. Their immense achievement has been helping to increase the average expectancy of life—to double it, in fact—by preventing or curing the diseases of infancy and early adulthood;

that is something quite different. Once a man or woman reaches 80, the prospect of living much longer is only a little better than it might have been in the 17th century (that is, if the octo then had adequate food and care). Has modern medicine added as much as two years to his prospective span? Gerontologists are trying to add more, and they have found some promising guides to future research—for instance, the notion that brain damage in later life may be partly the result of a virus—but so far those guides have not led to practical results. Methods have been found, however, to alleviate various infirmities of age, including broken hips and blocked aortas. Perhaps in the future our active lives, or those of persons a little younger, may be lengthened almost to the end of our days on earth; that is the most we can hope for. Otherwise we remain subject to the edicts of the god Terminus.

And what are those edicts? A different one seems to govern the span of each individual, depending largely on his genes, but also on his lifestyle and his chosen profession. As for the average, if any, we can only look at past records and make a guess. My own guess would be that without grave diseases or crippling accidents or inherited defects, and with a careful diet, the normal human life span might be about 90 years—a little more for women, a little less for men. Centenarians would seem to be a breed apart, marked from their earliest days. Almost all of them come from long-lived families. In age they are more cheerful than others, so doctors report, and their clinical records show very few serious illnesses. Much as we others might like to emulate them, we cannot join their company by striving.

TURNING again to the past, we find that great artists, if they didn't die in early manhood—not womanhood, for there were few famous women in the arts before the 19th century—may have longer productive lives than those in other callings. Sophocles is one of the earliest confirmed examples. When he was 89, his oldest son brought suit against him in an Athenian court; the son claimed that Sophocles had fallen into his dotage and was unable to manage his estate. As evidence in his defense, Sophocles read aloud to the court a draft of the tragedy on which he was working; it was *Oedipus at Colonus*, one of the two great plays about age, the other being *King Lear*. The judges instantly rose, dismissed the suit, and escorted the poet to his home. "Poets die young," we hear it said, but if they survive into middle age they are likely to prove a long-resistant species. In our own century some poets have lived about as long as Sophocles and have continued working to the end; I think of Hardy, Frost, Sandburg, and my friend John Hall Wheelock, who wrote his best poems after he was 80 and had a new book half finished when he died at 91.

Painters and sculptors sometimes have very long productive lives. Here the familiar examples, besides Goya, are Titian, Michelangelo, Monet, Matisse, Chagall—and of course Picasso, who said, "Age only matters when one is aging. Now that I have arrived at a great age, I might just as well be 20." Shortly before his death at 91, he was still venturing into new fields of art. In the American Academy of Arts and Letters, the oldest member (as I write) is a sculptor, José de Creeft, 94. The second oldest is a painter, Georgia O'Keeffe, 91, who has produced some admirable work in recent years.

I have a feeling that novelists, to speak in general, are not a long-lasting breed, though I have to admit exceptions. E. M. Forster, Somerset Maugham, and P. G. Wodehouse all lived into their nineties and Rebecca West is still dispensing wisdom at 87. Many others, however, must have followed the example of Balzac and Dickens; they shortened their time on earth by living hypertensively in their imaginations. Among the truly great, a small company, Tolstoy was the only one to live beyond 80. In my World War I generation of writers, all the famous novelists have vanished, beginning with Thomas Wolfe at 37 and Scott Fitzgerald at 44 (I omit Henry Miller, now 88, who is more and less than a novelist). The other survivors are Archibald MacLeish, Lewis Mum-

ford, Kenneth Burke, and E. B. White, all octogenarians. "We are the last leaves on the oak," Mac-
Leish wrote me. Those last leaves are essayists or
poets, two breeds that seem to outlast fiction
writers.

Musicians are an even hardier breed, as note
among others Toscanini, Casals, and Arthur Ru-
binstein, who gave a concert at 89, when his vision was so impaired that he could no longer read
music or even distinguish his fingers on the key-
board. He played entirely from memory and crit-
ics said he played better than ever. Eubie Blake,
the black composer, still performs in public at 96.

Scientists, mathematicians, and philosophers
seem to be long-enduring: Santayana lived to be
88; John Dewey and Bertrand Russell survived
well into their nineties. Doctors have a shorter
life expectancy, on the average and with many
exceptions (the one I mentioned, the famous in-
ternist who retired at 94, is Burrill Crohn, now of
South Kent, Connecticut). Apparently most of
his colleagues drove themselves too hard.

I note that many lawyers outlast the members
of other professions. One of them, an octogenarian with all his buttons, said at a testimonial dinner for his senior partner, "They tell you that
you'll lose your mind when you grow older.
What they don't tell you is that you won't miss it
very much." Often the lawyers who live longest
are those who become judges. "If you want to live

forever," Felix Frankfurter used to say, "get yourself appointed to the Supreme Court." Justice Frankfurter died at 83, a few years after he stepped down from the bench. Justice Holmes lived until a few days before his 94th birthday. Besides the sounder reasons for his being remembered, there is the classical remark he made on catching sight of a pretty girl: "Oh, to be 80 again!"

A general rule might be that persons called upon to give sage advice—unless they are doctors—live longer than persons who act on that advice; thus, corporation lawyers and investment bankers live longer than the presidents of corporations. The presidents, as a group, have a hard time adjusting themselves to retirement at 65. "They drink too much," a fiction writer said of them. But fiction writers as a group also drink too much.

Those matters of comparative longevity among sexes, races, and professions are not my present concern. Like many old people—or so it would seem from various reports—I think less about death than might be expected. As death comes nearer, it becomes less frightening, less a disaster, more an everyday fact to be noted and filed away. There is still what John Cowper Powys, in his book *The Art of Growing Old*, calls "the central miracle of being alive." The question that obsesses me is what to do with those 6.7 years, more

or less, that the Census Bureau has grudgingly al-
lowed me.

TO speak in general terms, old people would like
to have a clearly defined place and function in
American life; it is something they now lack.
Their function was more widely recognized in
many primitive societies, especially those which
hadn't acquired the art of writing. Nothing of the
past survived there unless it was remembered by
old persons, those who had mastered the lore of
the tribe, its rites, customs, legends, genealogies,
and means of coping with sudden dangers. They
were the tribal libraries, repositories of knowl-
edge which they jealously guarded and passed
along to younger persons only in return for gifts.
They also served as priests and medicine men,
since they were thought to be closer to the realm
of spirits. Feared and honored in this role, they
received still other gifts, so that they often ended
with more possessions than warriors in the prime
of life.

There were other tribes less bent on maintain-
ing social stability—or simply with less to eat—in
which older persons were ordinarily starved or
abandoned in the wilds. Indeed, the aged enjoyed
or suffered every variety of treatment in the primitive world, from being obeyed and venerated to
being cast from a high rock into the sea, as among

the ancient Scythians. Still, there are a few generalities to be hazarded. Older persons were usually better treated in agricultural societies, where there was some work they could do almost to the end; if they couldn't any longer plow a field, they could pull weeds or mind the children. The situation was different among hunting and food-gathering tribes, which had to move about a great deal; often they left old people behind as encumbrances. Another generality: tribes that mistreated their children also mistreated the aged, since they had never formed bonds of affection between generations. Tribes that petted children were usually kind to their older members—though sometimes that kindness took the form of putting them to death in a tender fashion. "Dear Father!" an Eskimo's daughter cried out to him after the neighbors had encouraged him to jump into the sea. "Push your head under the water. That way the road will be shorter."

Old persons lost one of their functions when tribal lore was committed to writing; their store of memories became less essential to the community. They gained in status, however—or a few of them gained—when property relations were stabilized, for the simple reason that the able or grasping ones had accumulated fortunes that were protected by law. Having the power of the purse, they often tyrannized over their wives, children, and dependents. That power might be extended to larger communities, some of which came to be ruled over by old men, by *gerontes*. Thus, in Sparta a central governing body was the gerousia, or council of elders, composed of chosen men over 60, who served for life; it proposed laws to the general assembly and conducted trials that involved capital crimes. In Rome the senate was at first a council of elders composed of former magistrates. It exercised its greatest power during the middle years of the Roman republic and declined in importance during the civil wars of the last two centuries before Christ. Its decline suggests another generality: that older persons (always of the privileged classes) are likely to be most powerful in times of social stability, and weakest in times of rapid change and civil commotion. As for slaves and artisans, they do not figure in the historical records and, it would seem, did not often attain old age.

China, with the most stable society of historic times, showed a special respect for aged persons, not excluding mothers-in-law. In Europe during the Middle Ages, the old played no great part in public life; they were few in number and society was so unsettled that boldness and a sharp sword were more important than accumulated wisdom. Venice had more stability than other European cities, and there the doges, who served as ceremonial heads of state, were almost always old men. The most famous doge, Enrico Dandolo, assumed office at 85 and retained it until his death at 97. Personal distinction gave him a degree of real power, but most of the doges simply obeyed the Council of Forty (later the secret Council of Ten), also consisting of old men. France during the restoration of the Bourbons, 1814–1830, was another gerontocracy; it had only 90,000 electors, for the most part elderly men of property, and only 8000 who were qualified to hold office—all of these, a pamphleteer asserted, "asthmatic, gouty, paralytic beings who have no wish for anything except peace and quiet."

For the middle classes, age had its comforts and compensations during the 19th century. It was an era of family businesses, often with a patriarch at the head of them, a man unwilling to share authority and waiting till the last moment before passing the business over to a middle-aged son. It was a time when there were more peasants in Europe, more small independent farmers in America, and it would seem that men (not always women) last longer in agricultural societies. Families were more cohesive then and tried to take care of their own members, including grandparents and maiden aunts; people expected to die at home. But the century was less kind to the millions without resources and without a family. In age they were "on the county" or "on the town," and what they dreaded was dying in the poorhouse.

OUR own era has a mixed record as regards its treatment of what are now called senior citizens; it takes care of them after a fashion. Government agencies, federal and state, have assumed many of the functions that used to be performed in a haphazard fashion by families and neighborhoods. Social Security, Medicare, and food stamps are fairly recent measures, and it is hard now to see how the country did without them for so many years. But meanwhile the older population keeps increasing; by 1978 there were 23.5 million Americans over 65. Under present arrangements they have to be supported by the productive labor force, or by savings accumulated during their own productive years, and the number of persons between 20 and 65 is not increasing at the same rate. Soon there will be greater burdens on the labor force, and the country is not so fabulously rich as it seemed to be in the early years after World War II; it has less to sell abroad and more to import at rising prices.

If we judge by earlier examples, this is not one of the eras when older people might expect to be honored and cherished. They have fared best, as we have seen, in agricultural or trading societies, in settled communities that remembered the past, and in periods of relative social stability. Ours is a period of frantic changes when memories have become irrelevant; when experience is less to be valued than youthful force and adaptability. It is a long time since the country might have been described as basically agricultural; now our lives, in some respects, have come to resemble those of the hunting or food-gathering tribes. Like them we wander over the face of the land; like them we regard the old as encumbrances to be left behind or sent off to die in what we think is a safe haven.

This has been an age of migrations: from countryside to city to suburb (and often back to countryside, but not to be farmers again); from Snowbelt to Sunbelt, and, for the old, from New England to Florida, from Iowa to Arizona. Once-vigorous communities have lost their sense of cohesion and their local pride. How long is it since people boasted of living in Cleveland ("Sixth City," as it used to advertise in *The Saturday Evening Post*) or Bridgeport or Detroit? Neighborliness is a fading ideal. Who would admit to being pious, in the Latin sense of being dutiful toward one's parents, relations, and native country (like *pius Aeneas*)? The household altar, *ara domestica*, has been dismantled and the family silver sold by the ounce. Family ties are coming to depend on the long-distance telephone. With childlessness and impermanent marriages, it is easy to predict that many persons now in their thirties will have a lonely old age.

To make things more difficult for those now in their sixties, or beyond, the era is one of financial confusion when thrift and foresight, those qualities of the old, are no longer sure of being rewarded. So you bought absolutely safe bonds in

1968 to prepare for your later years? At this moment the bonds are worth two-thirds or less of
the dollars you paid for them, and the punctual
income they yield will buy only half as much as
in the beginning. Or you invested in real estate
that you thought was certain to increase in value?
Usually it did increase, but now you can't afford
the redoubled taxes or meet payments on the
mortgage. Or you (not I) moved to Florida on
the assurance of what seemed a comfortable pen-
sion and now you can't live on it; you have to
apply for relief in a town full of strange faces. Or
again, your doctor has advised an operation and
you find that Medicare stops far short of paying
the hospital bill; where will the money come
from? Social Security is a great help, but it
doesn't offer a living wage, and the government
forbids you to rejoin the working force on pain of
not receiving its monthly stipend—that is, until
you are 73; then the government throws up its
hands and says, "All right, you've outlived our
calculations. Now get a job if you can."[2]

[2] To judge from Ronald Blythe's excellent book *The
View in Winter*—which appeared just as I was finishing
this manuscript—old people in England have a somewhat
better time of it than their American coevals. Medical care
costs them nothing, or next to nothing, and the social-secu-
rity system is more secure; at least the many old persons
whom Blythe interviewed had few complaints about it.
Even when living alone, they suffered less from the fear of
break-ins and muggings. More persons in each community

To get a job of any decent sort is the ideal of many, but the working force won't take you back. Nobody over 50 is easily hired; almost everyone not in government service is retired at 65 or 70, if he hasn't been discharged sooner (and no matter if he had been producing more than the younger person hired to replace him). Older persons are our great unutilized source of labor (don't tell me that there isn't work in this country for everyone to do; it simply doesn't get done). A growing weakness of American society is that it regards the old as consumers but not producers, as mouths but not hands. They aren't even first-rank consumers in a culture largely devoted to consumption, since they have fewer wants than younger people and less money to supply them. A study by the National Council on Aging reported that for persons over 65, average incomes were roughly half as large as for persons between 45 and 55.

Many of the retired do find work for themselves, paid or unpaid. They start new businesses, often based on their hobbies, or they do odd jobs of a special sort—sharpening saws, for example—

---

seemed honestly concerned with their welfare. But England has been no more successful than the United States in finding useful occupations for persons retired from industry. Many of them—so Blythe reports—spend most of their time looking out from the crack in their curtained window or sitting on the sea wall—the "front"—and watching the waves roll in.

or they form political groups to advance the welfare of others like themselves. Such persons are to be admired—and hurrah for the Gray Panthers and Maggie Kuhn! Others, however, let themselves be isolated in retirement communities or—often too soon—in nursing homes, where they are left without an occupation to dignify their lives. Their capabilities dwindle away like their bodies, through not being used.

I remember an old man dreaming on a bench in the Florida sun, outside his daughter's tourist cabin. From across the court I used to steal glances at him when my work wasn't going well. He sat with his workingman's big hands on his knees, stirring at moments to open and reflectively drain another can of beer, then drop it into a paper bag. He didn't raise his eyes when a flight of drunken robins went staggering through the air. Though he seemed happy enough as he sat there day after day, I thought he was abusing an old man's privilege of indolence. He may have felt that, with nothing better to do, drinking beer in the sun was a convenient form of euthanasia.

I DON'T want to voice complaints about the lot of the old. As a group we compose a disadvantaged minority, but some of us are vastly more fortunate than others. Although we are all in the same boat, with tickets for the same destination, we do not enjoy the same comforts during the voyage. The boat turns out to be an old-fashioned liner with first-, second-, and third-class accommodations, not to mention a crowded steerage. Age has inequalities that are even greater than those of youth. In the matter of income, for example, most of the old are well below the national median, but others are far above it. Many of the great American fortunes are now controlled by aged men (or by their widows or lawyers). It must be added, however, that those older fortunes are melting away, from the effect of inflation on conservative investments; almost all the growth is in new speculative fortunes.

It must also be added that mere wealth becomes less important in age, except as a symbol of power and security. Things harder to measure— health, temperament, education, esteem, and self-esteem—contribute more to one's life. Thus, intellectual poverty proves to be as bad as material poverty. The educated live better than the uneducated, even on similar incomes; they have more interests and occupations (for example, reading) and are entertained by prosperous friends. They may live longer, too, though it would be hard to quote statistics, and meanwhile they enjoy more respect.

Whether old people are truly respected by their neighbors, and by the world at large, is an-

other point at which their status differs. In our
present society they are usually pushed aside—
let's be frank about it—but there are stable small
communities, especially in the South and New
England, where some of them have a definite
place. A man of 90 in our little town was widely
consulted in questions having to do with titles,
boundaries, wills, and family connections. He
was impartial, he was truthful, and he served as
the walking memory of the tribe. When he died
a few years ago, his place was partly filled by a
woman, also in her nineties, who was compil-
ing a local history.

In college towns, many of which are stable
communities, there may be a retired professor,
one among many, or an almost-oldest living grad-
uate who becomes a cherished figure. That happened to a former colleague of mine, Bruce
Bliven, after he had a second heart attack and retired from his editorship of *The New Republic* in
1955. Editing a magazine had been his life, but he
found a new one. Moving west to Stanford, his
own college, he rented an apartment near the
campus and there he wrote every morning, as if
The New Republic's printer were waiting for
copy. He published three or four books, including an autobiography, *Five Million Words Later*,
which appeared when he was 80. Every afternoon, on doctor's orders, he went for a walk of
exactly two miles, measured by a pedometer. Almost everyone on the faculty came to know him

and smiled respectfully as he passed; he was their perambulating monument.

Bruce defended himself against old age in a special way, by making fun of it each year in a Christmas letter that went out to five hundred friends. In 1972 he said, "A year ago, when I was only 82, I wrote somebody that 'I don't feel like an old man, I feel like a young man who has something the matter with him.' I have now found out what it is: it is the approach of middle age, and I don't care for it." In 1973: "I am thinking of becoming an old man; if I decide to I'll send out cards and wear a lapel pin." In 1975: "We live by the rules of the elderly. If the toothbrush is wet you have cleaned your teeth. If the bedside radio is warm in the morning you left it on all night. If you are wearing one brown and one black shoe, quite possibly there is a similar pair in the closet.... I stagger when I walk, and small boys follow me making bets on which way I'll go next. This upsets me; children shouldn't gamble."

At the 1976 commencement, Bruce and Rosie, his wife of 63 years, were the oldest members present from the Stanford class of 1911, which was the oldest class represented. That year's Christmas letter was to be his last. He said in part, "I am as bright as can be expected, remembering the friend who told me years ago, 'If your I.Q. ever breaks 100, *sell*!' My motto this year is from the Spanish: 'I don't want the cheese, I only want to get out of this trap.' " Bruce could afford to make fun of himself, knowing that he was respected in the community.

He also profited from a situation that prevails in the arts and the learned professions, where so many younger people are trying to be first among their peers. Everyone striving for distinction is regarded as a rival and a potential enemy by everyone else engaged in the same struggle. Ambitious writers, painters, lawyers, scientists, and politicians have lived among professional jealousies since their apprentice days; they are used to being politely stabbed in the back; but if they survive to a fairly advanced age they find that most—not all—of the old vendettas have been interred. They have ceased to be rivals and are ticketed as hors concours, like some of the famous exhibitors at a world's fair. Any honors henceforth conferred on them will be honors to the whole profession.

One can imagine a young instructor saying, or feeling in his heart, "I won't make any more cracks about the old man. He's helping the rest of us now by presenting an image of achievement and durability. But let him take warning: he had better remain an image and not engage in literary or academic politics. For that we need more vigorous persons like myself. We'll use his name, we'll put him on the platform at meetings, out front, but we'll not invite him to our parties. Let him be like Emerson in his last ten years and serve as a benevolent effigy."

Among the truly great American writers, Emerson was the only one who resigned himself to occupying that position. Though he had lost his memory, everyone admired him for what he had written in his middle years. Everyone who approached him worshiped as at a shrine. Walt Whitman visited Concord in 1881, the year before Emerson died, and recorded an evening there in *Specimen Days*. "... without being rude, or anything of the kind," he says, "I could just look squarely at E., which I did a good part of the two hours. On entering, he had spoken very briefly and politely to several of the company, then settled himself in his chair, a trifle push'd back, and, though a listener and apparently an alert one, remain'd silent throughout the whole talk and discussion. ... A good color in his face, eyes clear, with the well-known expression of sweetness, and the old clear-peering aspect quite the same." Whitman was reverently gazing on the effigy of the Emerson that had been.

There have been writers high in the second rank who attained a similar position, and without losing their faculties: some names are Longfellow, Whittier, Julia Ward Howe, Robert Frost, and more recently Edmund Wilson. William Dean Howells had the position too, but was toppled from it at 70 by a revolt against the genteel tradition. At 78 he wrote to his friend Henry James, "I am a comparatively dead cult with my statues cut down and the grass growing over them in the pale moonlight." Each new generation elects its own heroes, and nobody can be certain who they will be. Besides, that Emersonian place as a revered idol is not a tempting goal for those, however ambitious, who are not much concerned with reputation. Those others don't want to be regarded as a monument to themselves, or a seemly model for the young, or a memory bank for scholars; they want to do their work—but at 80, what shall it be?

3

 I turn to books and find some guidance, but not so many firsthand reports as I had hoped to find. Very old people—I wonder why—have written comparatively little about the problems of aging. One exception is Florida Scott-Maxwell, whose last book, *The Measure of My Days*, is a record of her 83d year. That wasn't a lucky year for her. It was marked by a serious operation, by a recovery that was less complete than she thought, so that she collapsed after making a round of visits, then finally by the departure of beloved grandchildren for Australia. Living alone in a London flat, she came to terms with herself. "We who are old know that age is more than a disability," she says. "It is an intense and varied experience, almost beyond our capacity at times, but something to be carried high. If it is a long defeat it is also a victory, meaningful for the initiates of time, if not for those who have come less far."

She says, "When a new disability arrives I look about me to see if death has come, and I call quietly, 'Death, is that you? Are you there?' So far the disability has answered, 'Don't be silly, it's me.' " Somehow those words have the sound of being a sincere report, not a mere self-consolation, and as much can be said about her other statements.

She says, for example, "Age puzzles me. I thought it was a quiet time. My seventies were interesting and fairly serene, but my eighties are passionate. I grow more intense with age. To my own surprise I burst out with hot conviction. . . . I must calm down. I am too frail to indulge in moral fervour."

She says, giving sound advice, "A note book might be the very thing for all the old who wave away crossword puzzles, painting, petit point, and knitting. It is more restful than conversation, and for me it has become a companion, more, a confessional. It cannot shrive me, but knowing myself better comes near to that."

Almost at the end of the book she says, "I want to tell people approaching and perhaps fearing age that it is a time of discovery. If they say—'Of what?' I can only answer, 'We must find out for ourselves, otherwise it won't be discovery.' "

Florida Scott-Maxwell had a rich life behind her; she had been an actress, a housewife, an author, and for many years a consulting psychologist. She lived to be 95, still alone in her little flat, still visited and loved by her children and grand-children. In the field of writing about age she is an exception. The other four works I consulted were produced by men and women in their late fifties or early sixties, a time when most of them wanted to paint a bright prospect of their years to come; as yet they couldn't speak from experience.

Cicero's admired essay *De Senectute*, written when he was 62, is clearly a work of self-reassurance that praises the delights of age. At the same time it is a defense of the elder statesmen who composed the Roman senate. "The mightiest states," Cicero tells us, "have been overthrown by the young and supported and restored by the old." One might observe that his efforts and adages were wasted. Cicero was beheaded the following year, without having a chance to enjoy those promised delectations, and the senate he loved was gradually stripped of its powers. For two thousand years, however, his happily phrased maxims have been a comfort to elderly scholars. "Old age," he says in the guise of his spokesman, the aged Cato, "must be resisted and its deficiencies supplied by taking pains; we must fight it as we do disease." On memory: "I have never heard of any old man forgetting where he had hidden his money. The old remember every-thing that concerns them." On obeying nature (and still speaking through Cato): "I am wise in that I follow that good guide nature; it is not likely, when she has written the rest of the play well, that she should, like a lazy playwright, skimp the last act."

Emerson's essay "Old Age," written when he was 57, is still more optimistic and reassuring. He tries to make us believe that the years pour out their rewards as from a horn of plenty. "For a fourth benefit," he says, after listing three others, "age sets its house in order, and finishes its works, which to every artist is a supreme pleasure." But what if the house burns down, as Emerson's did a dozen years later, and what if the artist is left without enough strength of mind to finish the last of those inspiring essays? Emerson is one of my heroes, but often his observations lack the salt and sting of realism.

A Good Age, by Alex Comfort, appeared when its author was 56. It has the advantage of being written by a gerontologist, a man familiar with everything new in his field. "Gerontology," he says, "will not abolish old age; it will make it happen later." His book, which I recommend, is full of sound advice to the old, of a sort that wise doctors might give their patients in down-to-earth language. "What the retired need," he says, ". . . isn't 'leisure,' it's occupation. . . . Two weeks is about the ideal length of time to retire." Sometimes I suspect Alex Comfort of being too reassuring, as a tenderhearted doctor might be. Thus, he tries to banish one fear by asserting that dementia in age is neither general nor common, a statement that many would question from observation. He is cheery about the prospects for long-continuing sexual energy, this being his other special field (*The Joy of Sex*). Is he being tenderhearted about his own future, in the Ciceronian fashion?

Simone de Beauvoir is the least Ciceronian of the authors I read; she almost revels in a mood of bleak pessimism about everybody's future, including her own. *The Coming of Age*, a big book written when she was 60, presents a grim picture in almost every paragraph, except those dealing with some of her favorite artists. Even when speaking of these, she refuses to acknowledge—or hasn't yet discovered—that old age may have its inner compensations. Instead she drags existentialism out of the closet by quoting the abstruse remarks of her consort, Jean-Paul Sartre. One admires her, though, for bringing together the historical and literary records of old age as nobody else has done; here are facts to be brooded over. Incidentally, her book is a mine of fascinating anecdotes, some of which I have shamelessly borrowed. It was in *The Coming of Age* that I read about a famous 18th-century rake, the Duc de Richelieu, who at 84 took a young wife, gave her a child, and then deceived her with a bevy of actresses until he died at 92. Alex Comfort take note.

I WOULD not recommend the duke to my classmates as a model for Golden Age deportment.
Harvard '19 is my class, and, as a respite from
The Coming of Age, I took to reading what was
then its latest bulletin, dated May 1978. The class
had started with 722 members. When that bulletin appeared there were 208 survivors, all but a
handful of them octos. Only one showed any in-
clination to emulate the Duc de Richelieu—"and
my doctors," he said, "have forbidden me to
chase women unless they are going downhill."

Some fifty classmates contributed notes about
themselves to the bulletin. The general im-
pression I gathered was one of moderate activity
and moderate cheerfulness in accepting handi-
caps, almost the opposite of Beauvoir's grim
pictures. Frederic B. Whitman reported, for example, that he and his wife of fifty years were enjoying life "with great gusto," although he was
paraplegic. Whitman is a retired president of the
Western Pacific; he had started his career in rail-
roading as a freight-house trucker. It is to be
noted that our class had entered the labor market
during the Jazz Age, when individual success was
an almost universal ideal. A few of the classmates
had been grandly successful in business, and
none of those who reported was destitute. As Cicero himself conceded, "Old age is impossible to
bear in extreme poverty, even if one is a
philosopher."

The most cheerful were those who had recently enjoyed a family celebration, usually a golden wedding. One man wrote from the West Coast, "My wife and I celebrated our 50th by assembling a dozen of our children and grandchildren, with their mates. . . . We ourselves are in better condition than might be expected, although a bit creaky in the joints." Another wrote from Illinois, "My children and grandchildren gave me a big party on my 80th birthday. Had such a good time that I am looking forward to my 85th." I should have mentioned grandchildren among the solid pleasures of age. They are valued chiefly for themselves, but partly, it would seem, as an insurance policy against loneliness. The classmates sometimes boasted of the number of their grandchildren, as they didn't boast about having several sons and daughters. Great-grandchildren, if any, are valued largely as a form of reinsurance.

The most unhappy classmate was a man whose wife had recently died, leaving him alone, without occupation, in a rather large Arizona house—"Also I have been unable to drive a car for four years," he said. "Thank goodness for good friends." The old help each other. One classmate, a New England clergyman, was spending much of his free time "visiting the elderly in the various nursing homes and retirement centers. They are the forgotten ones," but he remembered.

It was refreshing to learn how many of the classmates hadn't retired. Richard L. Strout had been with *The Christian Science Monitor* since 1921, most of that time as head of its Washington bureau; in 1977 he was given a special Pulitzer award. Morton S. Enslin, a theologian, was still teaching at Dropsie University, many years after having been retired because of age from St. Lawrence University and then Bryn Mawr. He was hoping for more invitations to preach. Jacob Davis was president of a wholesale jewelry firm. He wrote from Pittsburgh, "I work five days a week. Without a daily job I'd be hard put to maintain my sanity." Several classmates had started new businesses: manufacturing cross-country skis, semicommercial gardening, selling out-of-print books by mail. "The day of the week never seems long enough," one man complained. "Do you have the time?" a young woman whispered to another '19er while she was sitting beside him in a doctor's waiting room. He whispered back, "Time for what?"

I was impressed by the second career of a banker and foundation executive. At 70 he had resigned his chairmanships and had taken up watercolor painting. He went back to school (as Goya said, "I am still learning"), painted hard, had exhibitions, and sold pictures. Had he been happy? I distrust that word, whose meaning is summed up for me in the phrase "happy as a clam." The point is that he had been leading a sort of work-filled afterlife on earth. For all my praise of indolence, which has its place in the old man's day, work has always been the sovereign specific.

In June 1979, a year after issuing that bulletin, the class held its sixtieth reunion. About sixty of the survivors were present, in spite of problems in getting to airports, and there was perhaps an equal number of wives and widows. "I like the women," my wife said. "You men are beginning to look alike." By then all the men were octos except Louis Dolan, the baby of the class, who was born in 1900 and entered Harvard at 15. Almost all of them looked hale and vigorous until they tried walking downstairs, and then they held on to the banisters. There wasn't so much drinking as at earlier reunions; the good-time Charlies had vanished. At a cocktail party the voices were animated, but low, friendly, and without the ring of self-importance. "Are you still buying and selling corporations?" somebody asked Roy Little, who was known for having organized Textron, Inc. "Not so many as before," he answered. "I've been writing a book and I'll bet you don't know the title."

"Somebody told me it was *How to Lose a Million Dollars.*"

"That was before inflation," Little said. "No, the title is *How to Lose $100,000,000 and Other Valuable Advice.*" He ruminated. "Of course that's a rough figure and I never lost a hundred million at one time. But over the last sixty years, if you count it up, I've lost a good deal more."

There was a pleasant dinner, with speakers, and a bus took us back to the hotel. Almost everyone went to bed early. I thought as I undressed that our glow of comradeliness was not unlike the mood of castaways on a beleaguered island, happy to have survived together, but waiting for another storm.

STORMS there will be, or at least darkening skies, and this by an edict of nature. We don't have to read books in order to learn that one's eighties are a time of gradually narrowing horizons. Partly the narrowing is literal and physical, being due to a loss of peripheral vision: "Incipient cataracts," the oculist says. Trees on a not-so-distant hillside are no longer oaks or maples, but merely a blur. It is harder to distinguish faces in a crowd—and voices too, especially if several persons are speaking at once. Would you like to see or hear more by drawing closer? Your steps are less assured, your sense of balance is faulty; soon you hesitate to venture beyond your own street or your home acres. Travel becomes more difficult and you think twice before taking out the car.

Your social horizons are also narrowing. Many of your old friends have vanished and it is harder to find new ones. Entertaining visitors and making visits have both become problems. You can't have many people in to dinner and hence you are invited out less often. More and more the older person is driven back into himself; more and more he is occupied with what goes on in his mind. "I am so busy being old," Florida Scott-Maxwell tells us, "that I dread interruptions." In middle age that absorption in the self had been a weakness to be avoided, a failure to share and participate that ended by diminishing the self. For the very old it becomes a pursuit appropriate to their stage in life. It is still their duty to share affection and contribute to the world as much as possible, but they also have the task of finding and piecing together their personalities. "It has taken me all the time I've had to become myself," Mrs. Scott-Maxwell says. Later she adds, "If at the end of your life you have only yourself, it is much. Look, you will find."

Often it seems that social justice for the aged is a neglected ideal, but there may be an approximate justice for individuals. At a time when so much depends on the past, those who have led rich lives are rewarded by having richer memories. Those who have loved are more likely to be loved in return. In spite of accidents and ingratitude, those who have served others are a little more likely to be served. The selfish and heartless will suffer most from the heartlessness of others, if they live long enough; they have their punishment on earth.

Even if the old are moderately cheerful, as a majority of my classmates reported themselves to be, I suspect that most of them are haunted by fears that they prefer not to talk about. One of the fears—I wonder how many have suffered from it—is that of declining into simplified versions of themselves, of being reduced from the complexity of adult life into a single characteristic. We have seen that happen to many persons in their last years. If they were habitually kind, in age they become, like Emerson, the image of benignity, and that is a happier fate than most. If they had always insisted on having their own way, in age they become masters or mistresses without servants—except perhaps a loving daughter—and tyrants without a toady. If they had always been dissatisfied, they become whiners and scolds, the terror of nursing homes. Everything disappears from their personalities except one dominant trait. They play traditional roles: the chatterbox, the fussbudget, the invalid, the hag, the hermit, the Langley Collyer, the secret drinker, the miser, the frightened soul, the bottom pincher, the maiden aunt, or the bachelor auntie; and they almost always look the part, as if the deep lines in their faces had been drawn by a makeup artist. It is frightening to think that one might end as a caricature of oneself.

There is a sharper fear, seldom discussed, that troubles many more old persons and sometimes leads to suicide. Does it explain why the suicide rate per 100,000 is higher among the aged? Obviously the fear is not of death; it is of becoming helpless. It is the fear of being as dependent as a young child, while not being loved as a child is loved, but merely being kept alive against one's will. It is the fear of having to be dressed by a nurse, fed by a nurse, kept quiet with tranquilizers (as babies with pacifiers), and of ringing (or not being able to ring) for a nurse to change one's sheets after soiling the bed. "My only fear about death," Mrs. Scott-Maxwell says, "is that it will not come soon enough. . . . Happily I am not in such discomfort that I wish for death, I love and am loved, but please God I die before I lose my independence."

The thought of death is never far absent, but it comes to be simply accepted. Often it is less a fear than a stimulus to more intense living. John Cowper Powys says, "The one supreme advantage that Old Age possesses over Middle Age and Youth is its nearness to Death. The very thing that makes it seem pitiable to those less threatened and therefore less enlightened ages of man is the thing that deepens, heightens, and thickens out its felicity." I am quoting again from Powys's book *The Art of Growing Old*, published when he was 72 (he lived to be 90). His exclamatory style is hard for me to relish, but he says a few things worth remembering. One of them is, ". . . we poor dullards of habit and custom, we besotted and befuddled takers of life for granted, require the hell of a flaming thunderbolt to rouse us to the fact that every single second of conscious life is a miracle past reckoning, a marvel past all computation."

That "flaming thunderbolt" of imminent death sometimes rouses older persons to extraordinary efforts. I think back on a friend, the poet and scholar Ramon Guthrie, whose career was full of adventures, public rewards of a limited sort, and private frustrations. At the end he achieved a triumph, but only by force of will and only after the doctors had abandoned hope for him.

I MET Ramon Guthrie on shipboard in the summer of 1923, when he was coming back to the States with his French wife. He was a tall, loose-framed young man who carried his head bent forward and sometimes peered at you from under jutting eyebrows; later a friend described him as having "the look of a genial hawk." He also had a Dick Tracy chin and a Great War flier's clipped mustache over a wide, sensitive mouth. Marguerite, his wife, was a blue-eyed woman from Lorraine, compact and sensible, who tried not to reveal that she was terrified at starting life in a new country, with no resources except what remained of her husband's disability pay. Ramon, though, had pushed his worries aside. Someday a great poem was certain to make him famous (or might it be a novel?). Until that time he could support himself and Marguerite in one fashion or another, perhaps by finding a teaching post at some university.

I learned something about his early life in conversation. Ramon had gone to work in a New England factory at 13, after spending part of his boyhood in an orphan asylum. A benefactor sent him to Mount Hermon Academy, then rigidly Protestant and evangelical, but he rebelled against the discipline and dropped out after three years of high school; that was the end of his American schooling. In 1916 he was working at the Winchester Arms factory in New Haven, then busy with war orders. He was accepted as a volunteer by the American Field Service, which had undertaken to man and equip ambulance sections for the French Army. With a detachment of Yale undergraduates, also volunteers, he sailed for Bordeaux on Christmas Day, three weeks before his 21st birthday. That was the start of a new career for him.

Not one of his future adventures or efforts was to be unique, except the very last; all the rest can be illustrated from the lives of other American writers, famous or forgotten, who were born at about the same time. There was, for example, driving an ambulance for a foreign army and later enlisting in American aviation. There was a wound that would never let him forget his war service. There was fascination with French life and with French women. There was helping to edit a little magazine, then publishing a first book of poems (a good one, but it went unnoticed). There was trying to support himself as a novelist and having two books praised by reviewers (but failing to complete a third and a fourth because of writer's block, a problem not unknown to others). There was a career in university teaching and scholarship (other writers of his generation would embark on that career, but Ramon was a precursor). Finally there was the lifelong effort to create a work of art that might serve as a lasting testimony to all he had suffered and enjoyed. We might have learned about all those experiences in other lives—that is, if we read literary biographies—but Ramon Guthrie himself may have been unique in having undergone so many of them, and also unique in the intensity with which he confronted each new choice, as well as in the tricks of fate that followed.

Take, for example, what happened when he was still in bombing school. Fifty years later he wrote me about the adventure. "The second time," he says, "I got a chance to go up in a plane—it was a two-place Sopwith strut-and-a-half—the socket fell off the joystick at 300 meters and we spun into the ground with me in one half of the plane and the pilot in the other. I walked about three miles back to camp and came to in a hospital three days later." Ramon went on with his training, though something had changed for him. He had given himself up for dead, and I suspect that he came to regard himself as, in effect, leading a

posthumous life. It would seem that many aviators who survived the Great War had the same
feeling; "All the Dead Pilots" William Faulkner
was to call them. In Ramon's case the first mishap
was to be compounded by what amounted to a
second death.

This was on September 18, 1918, in a bombing
raid over the village of La Chaussée. The raid was
a classical instance of military arrogance and in-
eptitude. Ramon had been assigned to the Eleventh Bombing Squadron, which flew slow and
obsolete British planes; they were De Havilland
Fours, known to aviators as "flaming coffins"
from their habit of burning in the air if a bullet
hit the gas tank. German fliers used them to fatten
their records when they were looking for easy
kills. The Eleventh Squadron had survived till
then by never venturing over the lines except
with a strong fighter escort. In September it received a new commanding officer, a plump major
who belonged to a booster club back home and
had an appetite for glory.

"You boys have been playing it safe," the
major said. "Tomorrow you're going over the
lines and show the Huns what American aviators
are made of." He didn't order a fighter escort and,
in substance, he was pronouncing a death sen-
tence on each man in the formation.

The story of what followed I have heard from
various sources, always with different details. It is
safest to let Ramon speak for himself, as he was to

do in that letter written fifty years later. "We had been kept on alert," the letter says, "standing by our planes since 4 a.m. Then some thirteen hours later, about 5 p.m., the raid was canceled. After we had dispersed we were called back and ordered to make this improvised raid. No time to try out our machine guns"—most of which didn't work—"or get any briefing. We didn't even know what there was to bomb at La Chaussée. About eight planes took off. Two of them got lost in the clouds and dropped out; they were the lucky ones. It's a wonder we all didn't collide in the clouds.

"The rest of us were jumped by, I think, 19 red-nosed Fokkers. They were supposed to be Von Richthofen's former outfit (the Red Baron was dead by then). It was a game of ducking into the clouds and having the Germans dive down on us as we emerged from one cloud and headed for another. All the other planes in the formation were shot down. I got two Germans; they were later confirmed, as were two others before the war was over."

When Ramon's plane got back to the field as the first (except for the two strays) and the last to return, the go-getting major came bustling out to greet him. A story I have heard more than once is that Ramon opened up on him with the machine gun and then slumped forward in a faint. Ramon's letter makes the episode less dramatic. "When we landed," he says, "I think that I did release a couple of shots in the general direction of the major. He was shortly promoted colonel and sent to the rear."

Ramon's academic career is also a story with a curious twist, considering that he was a dropout from high school. How did he get his start as a distinguished professor? The army helped him in this instance; it sent him to the Sorbonne for one term, in 1919, before sending him home to languish in a series of military hospitals (this as a delayed result of his fall in the strut-and-a-half Sopwith). From the last of the hospitals he was released with a 100-percent disability rating. He found himself a job as a waterfront detective, but after six months of sleuthing he went back to France, this time with a subvention from the Veterans Bureau. Having friends, former aviators, at the University of Toulouse, he decided to follow them. That proved to be a happy choice, since Toulouse was then eager to have American students and didn't pay close attention to their academic transcripts. Ramon studied hard and, in a little more than two years, he acquired not only the *licence* (roughly equivalent to an M.A.) but also a doctorate "of the university." The latter degree was not highly regarded in France (as opposed to the doctorate "of the state," which took many years to earn), but in America it might help him to find an academic post.

Eventually he found the post, and then a better one, after misadventures that are not essential to the story. Let me vault ahead by forty years to another crisis, the one that followed his retirement as a full professor at Dartmouth in 1963. Ramon was writing poems again, after a series of detours through fiction, translation, scholarship (two masterly introductions to modern French literature), and painting, not to mention two wartime years as a captain, then a lieutenant colonel, in the Office of Strategic Services. At Dartmouth and elsewhere he was best known for his yearly seminar on Marcel Proust, one that attracted the brightest students. "Read Proust, don't study him" was the adjuration with which he began the course each fall. Ramon had followed his own precept; he had reread *Remembrance of Things Past* each year, 31 times in all, not skipping any of its million-and-a-quarter words, and each time discovering something new that he might subtly encourage his students to rediscover; he could be proud of the achievement. He could also be proud of the new poems, which were more personal than those he had written as a young man and were finding a wider audience. Not one of them, though, was the masterpiece of which he continued to dream, and meanwhile, year by year, his health was failing disastrously.

One day (or night, he couldn't tell) he came to himself in the intensive-care unit of the Dartmouth hospital. He had undergone an emergency operation for cancer of the bladder and the doctors thought he was dying. Lying there in "this frantic bramble of glass and plastic tubes and stainless steel"—those were his words for it—he suffered from hallucinations. "I am Marsyas," he told a nurse. Marsyas was the satyr, gifted at playing the double flute, who dared to challenge the god Apollo to a musical competition. For his presumption he was flayed alive and his hide was left on a thornbush in Thessaly. Ramon felt that he too had been flayed alive, but he still had work to do and fought against slipping into a coma. In what seemed to be his final hours he was composing poems in his head; perhaps the effort was what kept him alive. Later, when his fingers were strong enough to hold a pencil, he scribbled out the poems and friends carried them away to be typed, while Ramon worked forward on others.

He was reviewing his past: the rebellion at school, his mother's suicide in the charity ward of a New Haven hospital, the adventure in the clouds over La Chaussée, his friendship with heroes of the French Resistance, his loves, his despair, his aspirations, everything that mattered. A book had taken shape, if only in his head, before he was not so much released as reprieved from the hospital. It was to be a unified work, in effect a single very long poem, but this would be composed of many shorter poems in violently contrasting moods:

> Blessèd incongruities,
> blends of majesty and bawdry, tenderness and
>   horror—
> and innocence.

Ramon even had a title for the book: *Maximum Security Ward*. There was actual writing still to be done—rewriting too—but the book could be hurried through the press so the author would be alive to read the reviews. Some of these were long and enthusiastic, though there were not so many of them as the book deserved. Hardly anyone mentioned that Ramon had completed a project undertaken in youth, sometimes deferred for years, but never abandoned. At the very end, as it seemed, poking among the rubble of his days, he had discovered a lasting shape, the work of art for which he had always been seeking.

When *Maximum Security Ward* was published in 1970, the poet was still believed to be on the point of death. But life has a way of blunting its climactic moments, and Ramon survived three years longer. In 1971 Dartmouth gave him the honorary doctorate he had long deserved. I congratulated him on a visit that summer, and I also said, in the fashion of old friends, "Ramon, what you should have asked for was a high-school diploma."

4

 I don't propose Ramon Guthrie as a model that many of us would be able to follow, or wish to follow. He suffered vastly more than others from a feeling that some grand task was still and always to be accomplished. Even after completing his final work, he continued to struggle against nature. He couldn't bear saying to himself what most of us hope to say at the end: "It is time to rest." Still, there is a lesson in his career, one that is reinforced in a modest fashion by the testimonies of my classmates. Poet or housewife, businessman or teacher, every old person needs a work project if he wants to keep himself more alive.

It should be big enough to demand his best efforts, yet not so big as to dishearten him and let him fall back into apathy. But otherwise what sort of project? There is a wide choice within the limits of one's interests and capabilities. The project can be an old one based on the less taxing

side of one's earlier career (the trial lawyer becoming a consultant), or it can be an outgrowth
of some former hobby, or again it can be something completely new. Perhaps a new project is
better, since it calls upon aspects of the personality that were formerly neglected and hence may
release a new store of energy. It doesn't have to
cost money. A man in his late eighties writes me
from Iowa, "I am guilty of accumulating things
—not the rubbish you speak of and not useless to
me—I recycle them into works of art—even take
prizes with them. But if I should go suddenly,
somebody is going to have a huge bonfire. I am an
artist of a sort (as I wasn't before) and really expect some useful years yet."

I like to hear about bankers who—as did my
classmate—turn to painting after they are 70.
And what about Grandma Moses, the housewife
of Eagle Bridge, New York, who began painting
in oils at 78, when she found that her fingers were
too arthritic to hold a needle? Conversely, there
have been painters and composers who waited till
almost the same age before revealing an unexpected talent for calculation. One poet I knew,
impecunious during most of a long and distinguished career, took to speculating in Wall Street.
He amassed a small fortune before he died at 83.

Carl Sandburg continued writing poems well
into his eighties, but he also raised goats in North
Carolina. Katharine S. White, long respected as
the fiction editor of *The New Yorker*, retired to

Maine with her husband, the essayist E. B. White, and grew flowers. Each fall until the last, she planned and supervised the planting of bulbs in her garden. "As the years went by and age overtook her," the husband writes in his introduction to her posthumous book, *Onward and Upward in the Garden*, "there was something comical yet touching in her bedraggled appearance on this awesome occasion—the small, hunched-over figure, her studied absorption in the implausible notion that there would be yet another spring, oblivious to the ending of her own days, which she knew perfectly well was near at hand, sitting there with her detailed chart under those dark skies in the dying October, calmly plotting the resurrection."

Very often an old person's project has to do with things that live on and are renewed: gardens, orchards, woods, or a breed of cattle. He counsels and supervises long after he has become, like Katharine White, unable to dig or harvest. "He plants trees to profit another age," Cicero quotes an earlier Latin author as saying, and himself continues, "If you ask a farmer, however old, for whom he is planting, he will reply without hesitation, 'For the immortal gods, who intended that I should not only receive these things from my ancestors, but also transmit them to my descendants.'" The welfare and renewal of the family is a very ancient project for old persons, one that has led to follies and disasters over the centuries, but also, as we often forget, to solid rewards. Families, whether illustrious or obscure, have maintained themselves in a surprising fashion.

In the present age family ties have frayed and broken, even if some of them remain stronger than many people believe. More and more old persons have transferred their hopes, in whole or part, to some other social stucture. "Colby College is my family," I heard an old bachelor say. More of the new projects (but many of the older ones too) have to do with a university, a church, a hospital, a community, or a cause. The very rich may endow museums that bear their names and testify enduringly to their love of art. A plaque in a hospital corridor attests that this wing or ward is owed to the generosity of, let us say, Mrs. Roberta Jones. Will she be remembered? At least she hopes to exert a good influence on others from beyond the grave.

Artists in general have the strongest desire to fashion something whose life will be self-contained and independent of their own mortality; that explains why so many of them work furiously at their projects to the end. But can't we all be artists, each in his own fashion?

ONE project among many, one that tempts me and might be tempting to others, is trying to find a shape or pattern in our lives. There are such patterns, I believe, even if they are hard to discern. Our lives that seemed a random and monotonous series of incidents are something more than that; each of them has a plot. Life in general (or nature, or the history of our times) is a supremely inventive novelist or playwright, but he—she?—is also wasteful beyond belief and her designs are hidden under the Langley Collyer rubbish of the years. She needs our help as collaborators. Can we clear away the bundles of old newspapers, evading the booby traps, and lay bare the outlines of ourselves?

Those outlines, if we find them, will prove to be a story, one with a beginning, a development, a climax of sorts (or more than one climax), and an epilogue. John Cowper Powys says in one of his vatic moments, "... in only one way can our mortal and, it may be, our immortal life be bravely, thoroughly, and absolutely justified, and that way is by *treating it as a story*." He might better have said, "... as a drama for each of us in which he or she has been the protagonist." Not only that; we have been the audience too, and perhaps the critic planning his report for a morning paper: "The leading character was played by _____" (insert your name), "who was no more than adequate in his difficult role." Or was he better than merely adequate, or worse, much worse? In age we have the privilege—which sometimes becomes a torture on sleepless nights—of passing judgment on our own performance. But before passing judgment, we have to untangle the plot of the play.

A first step in the untanglement, if we choose to make that effort, is gathering together the materials that composed our lives (including even the rubbish, which may prove to be more revealing than we had suspected). In other words, the first step is simply remembering. That seems easy in the beginning, since it always starts with our childhood, whose scenes are more vividly printed on our minds. Some of them, though, may reappear unexpectedly—for example, in my case, the picture of Jim Overman taking off his work shoes and insisting that I wear them on my bare feet before crossing the patch of nettles that barred our way to the farm lane. Jim followed me in heavy woolen socks that had been knitted for him by his older sister Maggie, who flashes across my mind as an image of blowsy kindness. What happened to dear Maggie? What happened to Jim after he went to work in a steel mill? Both of those orphans played their parts in my world.

Like many older persons, or so one suspects, I find myself leaping forward from childhood to recent years. These too are easy for most of us to remember, except in such matters as names and faces and where we mislaid our glasses. ("Thank goodness, you don't have to look for them anymore," a longtime neighbor phoned my wife to say. "I found them in the freezer compartment.") But the old, as Cicero said, end by recalling whatever really concerns them in the recent past. It is the middle years that prove hardest to recapture, so many of the persons and incidents having grown dim, but we can find the shape of these too, if we continue our efforts.

There are tangible aids to remembering, as notably letters, old snapshots, daybooks, and mementos, if we have saved them. Old tunes ring through our heads and some of them bring back pictures; this one was "our" song, Doris said, and you see the look on her face when she hummed the words. What became of Doris after she married somebody else and moved to California? And Mr. Wagner, the boss who used to dance the gazotsky at office parties? Characters crowd in on us, each making a contribution, and gradually our world takes shape. We tell stories about it, perhaps only to ourselves, and then arrange the stories in sequence: this must have been our second act and this was the third. All these efforts, if continued, might lead to an absolutely candid book of memoirs; old persons have nothing to lose by telling the truth. For others it might lead to nothing more than notebook jottings and advice to the young that might or might not be remembered. No matter: it is a fascinating pursuit in itself, and our efforts will not have been wasted if they help us to possess our own identities as an artist possesses his work. At least we can say to the world of the future, or to ourselves if nobody else will listen, "I really *was*"—or even, with greater self-confidence, "I was and am *this.*"